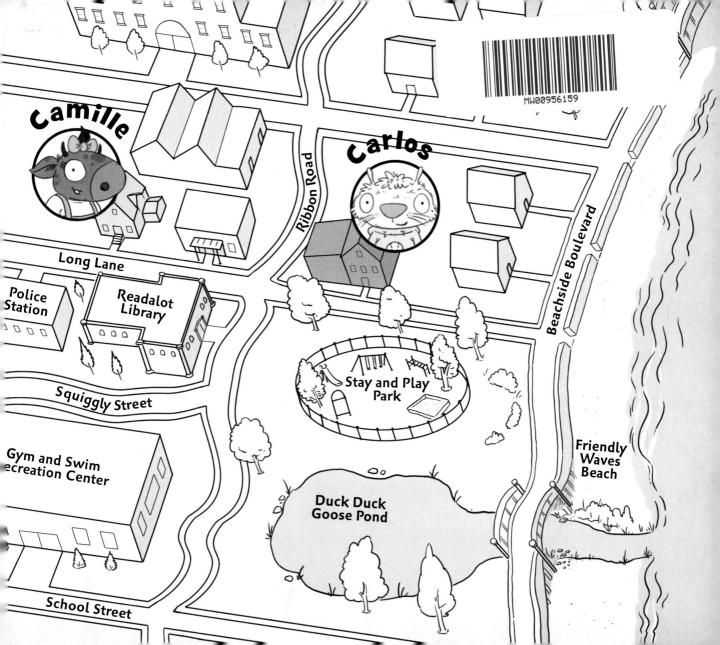

Stuart J. Murphy

Emma's Friendwich

Social Skills: Making Friends

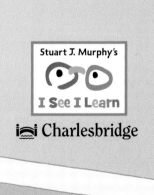

Stuart J. Murphy's
I See I Learn

🌉 Charlesbridge

Emma had just moved to a new house.

She loved her new room.

Pickle loved their new yard.

And they both loved their new street.

But Emma didn't have any new friends.
Not even one.

A girl Emma's age lived right next door.
Emma heard the girl's mother calling,
"Freda, it's time for lunch."
Freda answered, "I'm busy playing with Percy."
Emma wanted to play, too.

The next day Emma sat on her back porch,
eating her sandwich. She imagined a sandwich
made of friends—a FRIENDwich!

Then she saw Freda. She was all alone, too.
She was building a great big castle.

Emma looked at Freda. Freda looked up.
"Maybe if I **smile**," thought Emma.

She tried and tried.
Finally she could feel it.
She was smiling!
Freda smiled back.

smile

Then Freda kept on building.

"Maybe if I **ask**," thought Emma.

"Hi, my name is Emma.
May I play, too?" she asked.

ask

"Sure," said Freda.

Emma built a wall. Freda built a tower.
Neither one said a thing.

"Maybe if I **help**," thought Emma.

"Here's a block for your tower," she said. Freda nodded.

They started to build together.

help

It was still very quiet.

"Maybe if I **share**," thought Emma.

"Do you want to add my toys to the castle?" she asked. Freda smiled and said, "Yes."

share

Soon Percy arrived.
"Look!" said Freda. "We have a new **friend!**"

friend

Emma, Percy, and Freda played together.
Then Emma's daddy called, "Emma, come finish your lunch."
Freda got on one side of her. Percy got on the other.
They both gave Emma a squeeze.

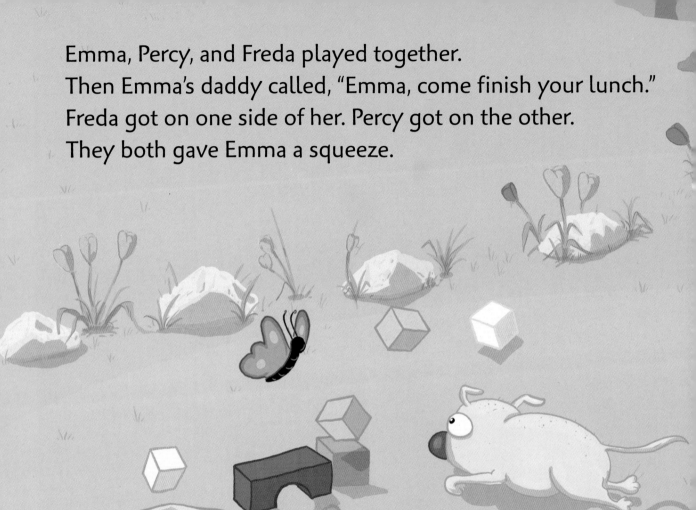

It was the best **friendwich** ever!

smile

ask

friends

share

help

A Closer Look

1. How do **you** make friends?

2. Name one of your friends. How did you become friends?

3. Look at the pictures. What are some things you can do when you want to make a friend?

4. What does someone do to make friends with you? Then what do you do?

5. Draw a picture. Show what you look like when you smile.

A Note About Visual Learning and Young Children

Visual Learning describes how we gather and process information from illustrations, diagrams, graphs, symbols, photographs, icons, and other visual models. Long before children can read—or even speak many words—they are able to assimilate visual information with ease. By the time they reach pre-kindergarten age (3–5), they are accomplished visual learners.

I SEE I LEARN™ books build on this natural talent, using inset pictures, diagrams, and highlighted words to help reinforce lessons conveyed through simple stories. The series covers social, emotional, health and safety, and cognitive skills.

Emma's Friendwich focuses on making friends, a social skill. The ability to make new friends is important as young children meet one another and work and play together.

Encourage your child to make a new friend!